1—

2/24

The Tale of Cupid and Psyche

D0198256

THE TALE OF
CUPID AND PSYCHE

Lucius Apuleius

Translated by Robert Graves

Illustrated by Roberta Arenson

Introduction by Marion Woodman

SHAMBHALA
Boston
1992

Shambhala Publications, Inc.
Horticultural Hall
300 Massachusetts Avenue
Boston, Massachusetts 02115

"Cupid and Psyche," from Apuleius' *The Golden Ass,* translated by Robert Graves. Copyright © 1951 by Robert Graves. Copyright renewed © 1979 by Robert Graves. Reprinted by permission of Farrar, Straus & Giroux, Inc.

Introduction © 1993 by Marion Woodman

All rights reserved. No part of this book may be reproduced in any form or by any means, electronic or mechanical, including photocopying, recording, or by any information storage and retrieval system, without permission in writing from the publisher.

9 8 7 6 5 4 3 2 1

First Edition
Printed in China on acid-free paper∞
Distributed in the United States by Random House, Inc.

Library of Congress Cataloging-in-Publication Data
Apuleius.
    [Psyche et Cupido. English]
    The tale of Cupid and Psyche / Lucius Apuleius: translated
  by Robert Graves: illustrated by Roberta Arenson.—1st ed.
      p. cm. ISBN 0-87773-888-2
    1. Psyche (Greek deity)—Fiction. 2. Cupid (Roman deity)—
Fiction. I. Graves, Robert, 1895– . II. Title.
PA6209.M5G73 1993 92-23306
873'.01—dc20   CIP

# Introduction

Marion Woodman

PARENTS, like the gods and goddesses of mythology, are divine before they are human. They are divine because as infants we are totally dependent upon them for life and nurture. Gradually, as we are weaned from that dependence, our parents descend from the Olympus upon which they were initially, unconsciously placed and move into a recognizable, conscious human state. They die into life, though traces of their original divinity remain in our unconscious.

A story about gods and goddesses is not

merely the preservation in fictional form of the infant's experience of total dependence, though some, including Freud, would reduce it to that. Divinity has survived the infancy of the race to become the ways in which we experience and understand ourselves as adults. In the highly ritualized forms of religion, divinity becomes at a conscious level an object of belief. The gods and goddesses move out of an infantile uncon-scious into adult consciousness to become the objects of faith and worship. Failing that, they are carried into adult consciousness, not as ob-jects of belief but as objects upon which (as in *The Tale of Cupid and Psyche*) we bestow what Coleridge called "a willing suspension of disbe-lief." Whether as objects of belief or "a willing suspension of disbelief," divinity is still within us, and is likely to remain within us so long as we remain in touch with our un-membered or re-membered selves. Divinity, like infancy, remains.

In the story of Cupid and Psyche, Venus is jealous of Psyche because the people have turned away from Her as an object of worship and are bestowing their adoration not upon a goddess to whom it belongs, but upon a mere mortal girl. In this turning from Venus to Psyche, from the divine to the human, an enormous shift in consciousness is being enacted. This shift is from the unconscious infancy of the race to the evolving consciousness that we identify with maturation and the suffering attendant upon it. The shift in the story is from the infant's world, wonderfully displayed in the playworld of Venus, to the adult world which Psyche painfully enters. She is preparing to replace Venus, the possessive and adoring mother of the spoiled son, Cupid, by becoming, at a conscious level, Cupid's wife. This process by which the mother is replaced by the wife is a fundamental human process. *The Tale of Cupid and Psyche* becomes less a story about gods and goddesses than a story about growing up.

Cupid, Venus, Vulcan, Jupiter, and Juno have long since disappeared from the Olympus they "once upon a time" inhabited. They have ceased to be gods and goddesses as such and have become psychological entities. They are mirror reflections of ourselves, mirrors in which we can reflect upon our own typical— or, if you like, archetypal—behavior. In Psyche's necessary interaction with them, she experiences her own essential growth from innocence through experience to the maturity which binds them together into what may be called a human identity. The gods and goddesses in the story of Cupid and Psyche die into human life. They become Psyche's slowly evolving experiential awareness of herself.

In this sense, they are not the divinities of our infancy or the infancy of the race. They are the mirrors which allow us to reflect upon our own psychic process, soul-custodians who help us to re-member who we are by conducting us to the inner places through which we have evolved and continue to evolve. Oddly enough, from a psychological perspective, they are still our guides. The story of Cupid and Psyche, recorded by Apuleius in the second century A.D.

in his picaresque novel, *The Golden Ass*, remains a psychological reflection of ourselves, as contemporary and new as if you who are now about to read it were its first reader.

The Tale of Cupid and Psyche

I

ONCE UPON A TIME there lived a king and queen who had three very beautiful daughters. They were so beautiful, in fact, that it was only just possible to find words of praise for the elder two, and to express the breathtaking loveliness of the youngest, the like of which had never been seen before, was beyond all power of human speech. Every day thousands of her father's subjects came to gaze at her, foreigners too, and were so dumbfounded by the sight that they paid her the homage due to the Goddess Venus alone. They pressed their right thumbs and forefingers together, reverently raised them to their lips and blew kisses towards her. The news of her matchless beauty spread through neighbouring cities and countries. Some reported: "Immortal Venus, born from the deep blue sea and risen to Heaven from its foam, has descended on earth and is now incarnate as a mortal at whom everyone is allowed to gaze." Others: "No, this time the earth, not the sea, has been impregnated by a heavenly emanation and has borne a new Goddess of Love, all the more beautiful because she is still a virgin." The princess's fame was carried farther and farther to distant provinces and still more distant ones and people made long pilgrimages over land and sea to witness the greatest wonder of their age. As a result, nobody took the trouble to visit Venus's shrines at Cyprian Paphos or Carian Cnidos or even in the isle of Cythera where her lovely foot first touched dry land; her festivals were neglected, her rites discontinued, the cushions on which her statues had been propped at her sacred temple feasts were kicked about the floor, the statues themselves were left without their usual garlands, her altars were unswept and cluttered with the foul remains of months-old burned sacrifices, her temples were allowed to fall into ruins.

When the young princess went out on her morning walks through the streets, victims were offered in her honour, sacred feasts spread for her, flowers scattered in her path, and rose garlands presented to her by an adoring crowd of suppliants who addressed her by all the titles that really belonged to the great Goddess of Love herself. This extraordinary transfer of divine honours to a mortal naturally angered the true Venus. Unable to suppress her feelings, she shook her head menacingly and said to herself: "Really now, whoever would have thought that I'd be treated like this? I, all the world's lovely Venus whom the philosophers call 'the Universal Mother' and the original source of all five elements! So I'm expected to share my sovereignty, am I, with a mortal who goes about pretending to be myself? And to watch my bright name, which is registered in Heaven, being dragged through the dirty mud of Earth! Oh, yes, and I must be content, of course, with the reflected glory of worship paid to this girl, grateful for a share in the expiatory sacrifices offered to her instead of me? It meant nothing, I suppose, when the shepherd Paris, whose just and honest verdict Jupiter himself confirmed, awarded me the apple of beauty over the heads of my two goddess rivals? No, it's quite absurd. I can't let this silly creature, whoever she may be, usurp my glory any longer. I'll very soon make her sick and sorry about her good looks: they are dead against the rules."

She at once called her winged son Eros, alias Cupid, that very wicked boy, with neither manners nor respect for the decencies, who spends his time running from building to building all night long with his torch and his arrows, breaking up respectable homes. Somehow he never gets punished for all the harm he does, though he never seems to do anything good in compensation. Venus knew that he was naturally bent on mischief, but she tempted him to still worse behaviour by bringing him to the city where the princess lived—her name, by the way, was Psyche—and telling him the whole story of the new cult that had grown up around her. Groaning with indignation she said: "I implore you, darling, as you love your mother, to use your dear little arrows and that sweet torch of yours against this impudent girl. If you have any respect for me, you'll give me my revenge, revenge in full. You'll see that the princess falls desperately in love with some perfect outcast of a man—someone who has lost rank, fortune, everything, someone who goes about in terror of his life and in such complete degradation that nobody viler can be found in the whole world."

She kissed him long and tenderly and then went to the near-by sea-shore, where she ran along the tops of the waves as they danced foaming towards her. At the touch of her rosy feet the whole sea suddenly calmed, and she had no sooner willed the powers of the deep to appear, than up they bobbed as though she had shouted their names. The Nereids were there, singing a part song; and Neptune, sometimes called Portumnus, with his blueish beard; his wife Salacia, the naughty goddess of the deep sea, with a lapful of aphrodisiac fish; and little Palaemon, their charioteer, riding on a dolphin. After these came troops of Tritons swimming about in all directions, one blowing softly on his conch-shell, another protecting Venus from sunburn with a silk parasol, a third holding a mirror for her to admire herself in, and a whole team of them, yoked two and two, harnessed to her car. When Venus goes for an ocean cruise she's attended by quite an army of retainers.

Meanwhile Psyche got no satisfaction at all from the honours paid her. Everyone stared at her, everyone praised her, but no commoner, no prince, no king even, dared to make love to her. All wondered at her beauty, but only as they might have wondered at an exquisite statue. Both her less beautiful elder sisters, whose reputation was not so great, had been courted by kings and successfully married to them, but Psyche remained single. She stayed at home feeling very miserable and rather ill, and began to hate the beauty which everyone else adored.

Her poor father feared that the gods might be angry with him for allowing his subjects to make so much of her, so he went to the ancient oracle of Apollo at Miletus and, after the usual prayers and sacrifices, asked where he was to find a husband for his daughter whom nobody wanted to marry. Apollo,

though an Ionian Greek and the true founder
of Miletus, chose to deliver the following oracle in Latin verse:

On some high mountain's craggy
     summit place
The virgin, decked for deadly nuptial rites,
Nor hope a son-in-law of mortal birth
But a dire mischief, viperous and fierce,
Who flies through aether and with
     fire and sword
Tires and debilitates all things that are,
Terrific to the powers that reign on high,
Great Jupiter himself fears this winged
     pest
And streams and Stygian shades his power
     abhor.

The king, who until now had been a happy man, came slowly back from the oracle feeling thoroughly depressed and told his queen what an unfavourable answer he had got. They spent several miserable days brooding over their daughter's fate and weeping all the while. But time passed, and the cruel oracle had to be obeyed.

The hour came when a procession formed up for Psyche's dreadful wedding. The torches chosen were ones that burned low with a sooty, spluttering flame; instead of the happy wedding-march the flutes played a querulous Lydian lament; the marriage-chant ended with funereal howls, and the poor bride wiped the tears from her eyes with the corner of her flame-coloured veil. Everyone turned out, groaning sympathetically at the calamity that had overtaken the royal house, and a day of public mourning was at once proclaimed. But there was no help for it: Apollo's oracle had to be obeyed. So when the preliminaries of this hateful ceremony had been completed in deep grief, the bridal procession moved off, followed by the entire city, and at the head of it walked Psyche with the air of a woman going to her grave, not her bridal bed.

Her parents, overcome with grief and horror, tried to delay things by holding up the procession, but Psyche herself opposed them. "Poor Father, poor Mother, why torment yourselves by prolonging your grief unnecessarily? You are old enough to know better. Why increase my distress by crying and shrieking yourselves hoarse? Why spoil the two faces that I love best in the world by crying your eyes sore and pulling out your beautiful white hair? Why beat your dear breasts until my own heart aches again? Now, too late, you at last see the reward that my beauty has earned you; the curse of divine jealousy for the extravagant honours paid me. When the people all over the world celebrated me as the New Venus and offered me sacrifices, then was the time for you to grieve and weep as though I were already dead; I see now, I see it as clearly as daylight, that the one cause of all my misery is this blasphemous use of the Goddess's name. So lead me up to the rock of the oracle. I am looking forward to my lucky bridal night and my marvellous husband. Why should I hesitate? Why should I shrink from him, even if he has been born for the destruction of the whole world?"

She walked resolutely forward. The crowds

followed her up to the rock at the top of the hill, where they left her. They returned to their homes in deep dejection, extinguishing the wedding-torches with their tears, and throwing them away. Her broken-hearted parents shut themselves up in their palace behind closed doors and heavily curtained windows.

Psyche was left alone weeping and trembling at the very top of the hill, until a friendly west wind suddenly sprang up. It played around her, gradually swelling out her skirt and veil and cloak until it lifted her off the ground and carried her slowly down into a valley at the foot of the hill, where she found herself gently laid on a bed of the softest turf, starred with flowers.

It was such a cool, comfortable place to lie that she began to feel rather more composed.

She stopped crying and fell asleep, and when she awoke, feeling thoroughly refreshed, it was still daylight. She rose and walked calmly towards the tall trees of a near-by wood, through which a clear stream was flowing. This stream led her to the heart of the wood where she came upon a royal palace, too wonderfully built to be the work of anyone but a god; in fact, as soon as she came in at the gates she knew that some god must be in residence there.

The ceiling, exquisitely carved in citrus wood and ivory, was supported by golden columns; the walls were sheeted with silver on which figures of all the beasts in the world were embossed and seemed to be running towards Psyche as she came in. They were clearly the work of some demi-god, if not a full god, and the pavement was a mosaic of all kinds of precious stones arranged to form pictures. How lucky, how very lucky anyone would be to have the chance of walking on a jewelled floor like that! And the other parts of the palace, which was a very large one, were just as beautiful, and just as fabulously costly. The walls were faced with massive gold blocks which glittered so brightly with their own radiance that the house had a daylight of its own even when the sun refused to shine: every room and portico and doorway streamed with light, and the furniture matched the rooms. Indeed, it seemed the sort of palace that Jupiter himself might have built as his earthly residence. Psyche was entranced. She went timorously up the steps, and after a time dared to cross the threshold. The beauty of the hall lured her on; and every new sight added to her wonder and admiration.

When well inside the palace she came on splendid treasure chambers stuffed with unbelievable riches; every wonderful thing that anyone could possibly imagine was there. But what amazed her even more than the stupendous wealth of this world treasury was that no single chain, bar, lock or armed guard protected it.

As she stood gazing in rapt delight, a voice suddenly spoke from nowhere: "Do these treasures astonish your Royal Highness? They are all yours. Why not go to your bedroom now, and rest your tired body. When you feel inclined for your bath, we will be there to help you—this is one of your maids speaking—and afterwards you will find your wedding banquet ready for you."

Psyche was grateful to the unknown Providence that was taking such good care of her and did as the disembodied voice suggested. First she found her bedroom and dozed off again for awhile, then she went to the bath, where invisible hands undressed her, washed her, anointed her and dressed her again in her bridal costume. As she wandered out of the bathroom she noticed a semi-circular table with a comfortable chair in front of it; it was laid for a banquet, though there was nothing yet on it to eat or drink. She sat down expectantly—and at once nectarous wines and appetizing dishes appeared by magic, floating up to her of their own accord. She saw nobody at all; the waiters were mere voices, and when someone came in and sang and someone else accompanied him on the lyre, she saw neither of them, nor the lyre either. Then a whole invisible choir burst into song. When this delightful banquet was over,

Psyche thought it must be about time to go to bed, so she went to her bedroom again and undressed and lay awake for a long time.

Towards midnight she heard a gentle whispering near her, and began to feel lonely and scared. Anything might happen in a vast uninhabited place like this, and she had fears for her chastity. But no, it was the whisper of her unknown husband.

Now he was climbing into bed with her. Now he was taking her into his arms and making her his wife.

He left her hastily just before daybreak, and almost at once she heard the voices of her maids reassuring her that though she had lost her virginity, her chastity was safe. So she went to sleep again.

The next day she made herself more at home

in her palace, and on the following night her invisible husband paid her another visit. The third day and night were spent in the same way until, as one might expect, the novelty of having invisible servants wore off and she settled down to what was a very enjoyable routine; at any rate she could not feel lonely with so many voices about her.

Meanwhile the old king and queen were doing exactly what she had asked them not to do—wasting their time in unnecessary grief and tears; and the news of Psyche's sad fate spread from country to country until both her elder sisters heard all the details. They left their palaces and hurried back in deep grief to their native city to console their parents.

On the night of their arrival Psyche's husband, whom she still knew only by touch and hearing, warned her: "Lovely Psyche, darling wife, the Fates are cruel: you are in deadly danger. Guard against it vigilantly. Your elder sisters are alarmed at the report of your death. They will soon be visiting the rock from which the West Wind blew you down into this valley, to see whether they can find any trace of you there. If you happen to hear them mourning for you up there, pay no attention at all. You must not answer them, nor even look up to them; for that would cause me great unhappiness and bring utter ruin on yourself."

Psyche promised to do as her husband asked; but when the darkness had vanished, and so had he, the poor girl spent the whole day in tears, complaining over and over again that not only was she a prisoner in this wonderful palace without a single human being to chat with, but her husband had now forbidden her to relieve the minds of her poor sisters, or even to look up at them without speaking. That night she went to bed without supper or bath or anything else to comfort her, and soaked her pillow with tears. Her husband came in earlier than usual, drew her to him, still weeping, and expostulated gently with her, "O Psyche, what did you promise me? What may I expect you to do next? You have cried all day and all evening and even now when I hold you close to me, you go on crying. Very well, then, do as you like, follow your own disastrous fancies; but I warn you solemnly that when you begin to wish you had listened to me, the harm will have been done."

She pleaded earnestly with him, swearing she would die unless she were allowed to see her sisters and comfort them and have a short talk with them. In the end she forced him to consent. He even said that she might give them as much jewellery as she pleased; but he warned her with terrifying insistence that her sisters were evil-minded women and would try to make her discover what he looked like. If she listened to them, her sacrilegious curiosity would mean the end of all her present happiness and she would never lie in his arms again.

She thanked him for his kindness and was quite herself again. "No, no," she protested, "I'd rather die a hundred times over than lose you. I have no idea who you are, but I love you. I love you desperately, I love you as I love my own soul; I wouldn't exchange your kisses for the kisses of the God Cupid himself. So please, please grant me one more favour! Tell your servant, the West Wind, to carry my sisters down here in the same delightful way that he carried me." She kissed him coaxingly, whispered love-words in his ear, wound her arms and legs more closely around him and called him: "My honey, my own husband, soul of my soul!" Overcome by the power of her love he was forced to yield, however reluctantly, and promised to give her what she asked. But he vanished again before daybreak.

II

MEANWHILE Psyche's sisters enquired their way to the rock where she had been abandoned. Hurrying there they wept and beat their breasts until the cliffs re-echoed. "Psyche! Psyche!" they screamed. The shrill cry reached the valley far below and Psyche ran out of her palace in feverish excitement, crying: "Sisters, dear sisters, why are you mourning for me? There's no need for that at all. Here am I, Psyche herself! Please, please stop that terrible noise and dry your tears. In a moment you'll be able to embrace me."

Then she whistled up the West Wind, and gave him her husband's orders. He at once obliged with one of his gentle puffs, and wafted them safely down to her. The three sisters embraced and kissed rapturously. Soon they were shedding tears of joy, not of sorrow. "Come in now," said Psyche, "come in with me to see my new home. It will make you both very happy." She showed them her treasure chambers and they heard the voices of the big retinue of invisible slaves. She ordered a wonderful bath for them and feasted them splendidly at her magical table. But this revelation of Psyche's goddess-like prosperity made them both miserably jealous—particularly the younger one, who was always very inquisitive. She was dying to know who owned all this fabulous wealth; so she pressed Psyche to tell her what sort of a man her husband was, and how he treated her.

Psyche was loyal to her promise and gave

away nothing: but she made up a story for the occasion. She said lightly that, oh, her husband was a very handsome young man, with a little downy beard, and spent all his time hunting in the neighbouring hills and valleys. But when her sisters began to cross-examine her she grew afraid. Suppose she contradicted herself or made a slip or broke her promise? She loaded them both with jewelled pins and rings, festooned them with precious necklaces, then summoned the West Wind and asked him to fetch them away at once. He carried them up to the rock, and on their way back to the city the poison of envy began working again in their hearts.

The elder said: "How blindly and cruelly and unjustly Fortune has treated us! Do *you* think it fair that we three sisters should be given such different destinies? You and I are the two eldest, yet we get exiled from our home and friends and married off to foreigners who treat us like slaves; while Psyche, the result of Mother's last feeble effort at child-bearing, is given the most marvellous palace in existence and a god for a husband, and doesn't even know how to make proper use of her tremendous wealth. Did you ever see such masses of amazing jewels, such cupboardsful of embroidered dresses? Why, the very floors were made of gems set in solid gold! If her husband is really as good-looking as she says, she is quite the luckiest woman in the whole world. The chances are that if he remains as fond of her as he is at present he will make her a goddess. And, my goodness, wasn't she behaving as if she were one already, with her proud looks and condescending airs? She's only flesh and blood after all, yet she orders the winds about and has a palaceful of invisible attendants. How I hate her! My husband's older than Father, balder than a pumpkin and as puny as a little boy; and he locks up everything in the house with bolts and chains."

"*My* husband," said the younger sister, "is even worse than yours. He's doubled up with sciatica, which prevents him from sleeping with me more than once in a blue moon, and his fingers are so crooked and knobby with gout that I have to spend half my time massaging them. You remember what beautiful white hands I used to have? Well, look what a state they are in now from messing about with his stinking fomentations and disgusting salves and filthy plasters! I'm treated more like a surgeon's assistant than a queen. You're altogether too patient, my dear; in fact, if you will excuse my saying so, you're positively servile, the way you accept this monstrous state of affairs. Personally, I simply can't stand seeing my youngest sister living in such undeserved style. I'm glad you noticed how haughtily she treated us, how she bragged of her wealth and how stingy with her presents she was. Then, the moment she got bored with our visit, she whistled up the wind and had us blown off the premises. But I'll be ashamed to call myself a woman, if I don't see that she gets toppled down from her pinnacle before long and flung into the gutter. And if you feel as bitter as you ought to feel at the way she's insulted us both, what about joining forces and working out some plan for humbling her?"

"I'm with you," said the elder sister. "And in the first place I suggest that we show nobody, not even Father and Mother, these presents of hers, and let nobody know that she's still alive. It's bad enough to have seen her revelling in her good luck, without having to bring the news home to be spread all over the place; and there's no pleasure in being rich unless people hear about it. Psyche must be made to realize that we're not her servants, but her elder sisters."

"Good," said the younger one. "We'll go back to our shabby homes and our shabby old husbands without telling Father and Mother anything. But when either of us thinks of a good plan for humbling Psyche's pride, let's come here again and boldly put it into operation."

The two bad sisters shook hands on this.

They hid the valuable presents that Psyche had given them and, as they neared their father's palace, each began scratching her face and tearing out her hair in pretended grief at having found no trace of their sister; which made the king and queen sadder than ever. Then they separated: each went back full of malicious rage to her own adopted country, thinking of ways for ruining her innocent sister, even if it meant killing her.

Meanwhile, Psyche's unseen husband gave her another warning. He asked her one night: "Do you realize that a dangerous storm is brewing in the far distance? It will soon be on you and unless you take the most careful precautions, it will sweep you away. These treacherous bitch-wolves are scheming for our destruction: they will urge you to look at my face, though as I have often told you, once you see it, you lose me for ever. So if these hateful vampires come to visit you again—and I know very well that they will—you must refuse to speak to them. Or, if this is too difficult for a girl as open-hearted and simple as yourself, you must at least take care not to answer any questions about me. Pretend that you have not heard them. This is most important, because we have a family on the way: though you are still only a child, you will soon have a child of your own which shall be born divine if you keep our secret, but mortal if you divulge it."

Psyche was exultant when she heard that she might have a god for a baby. She began excitedly counting the months and days that must pass before it was born. But she knew very few of the facts of life and could not make out why the mere breach of her maidenhead was having so odd an effect on her figure.

The wicked sisters were now hurrying to Psyche's palace again, with the ruthless hate of Furies, and once more she was warned: "Today is the fatal day. Your enemies are near. They have struck camp, marshalled their forces and sounded the 'Charge.' They are enemies of your own sex and blood. They are your elder sisters, rushing at you with drawn swords aimed at your throat. O darling Psyche, what dangers surround us! Have pity on yourself and on me and on our unborn child! Keep my secret safe and so guard us all from the destruction that threatens us. Refuse to see those wicked women. They have forfeited the right to be called your sisters because of the deadly hate they bear you. Forbid them to come here, refuse to listen to them when, like Sirens leaning over the cliff, they make the rocks echo with their unlucky voices. Preserve absolute silence."

Psyche, her voice broken with sobs, said: "Surely you can trust me? The last time my sisters came to visit me I gave you convincing proof of my loyalty and my power of keeping a secret; it will be the same again tomorrow. Only tell the West Wind to do his duty as before, and allow me to have a sight, at least, of my sisters; as a very poor consolation for never seeing you, my darling. These fragrant curls dangling all round your head; these cheeks as tender and smooth as my own; this breast which gives out such extraordinary heat; oh, how I look forward to finding out what you are really like by studying my baby's face! So please, be sweet and humour my craving—it will be bad for the baby if you refuse—and make your Psyche happy. You and I love each other so much. I promise that if you let me see them I won't be so frightened of the dark or so anxious to look at you when I have you safe in my arms, light of my life!" Her voice and sweet caresses broke down his resistance. He wiped her eyes dry with his hair, granted what she asked, and as usual disappeared again before the day broke.

The wicked sisters landed together at the nearest port and, not even troubling to visit their parents, hurried straight to the rock above the valley and with extraordinary daring leaped down from it without waiting for the breeze to belly out their robes. However, the West Wind was bound to obey standing orders, reluctant though he might be: he caught them in his robe as they fell and brought them safely to the ground.

They rushed into the palace crying: "Sister, dear sister, where are you?" and embraced their victim with what she took for deep affection. Then, with cheerful laughter masking their treachery, they cried: "Why, Psyche, you're not nearly so slim as you used to be. You'll be a mother before very long. We're dying to see what sort of a baby it's going to be, and Father and Mother will be absolutely delighted with the news. Oh, how we shall love to nurse your golden baby for you. If it takes after its parents, as it ought to, it will be a perfect little Cupid."

They gradually wormed themselves into her confidence. Seeing that they were tired, she invited them to sit down and rest while water was heated for them; and when they had taken their baths, she gave them the most delicious supper they had ever tasted, course after course of tasty dishes, from spiced sausages to marzipan, while an unseen harpist played for them at her orders, and an unseen flautist, and a choir sang the most ravishing songs. But even such heavenly music as that failed to soften the hard hearts of the sisters. They insidiously brought the conversation round to her husband, asking her who he was, and from where his family came.

Psyche was very simple-minded and, forgetting what story she had told them before, invented a new one. She said that he was a middle-aged merchant from the next province, very rich, with slightly grizzled hair. Then breaking the conversation off short, she loaded them with valuable presents and sent them away in their windy carriage.

As they rode home the younger sister said: "Now, what do you make of the monstrous lies she tells us? First the silly creature says that her husband is a very young man with a downy beard, and then she says that he's middle-aged with grizzled hair! Quick work, eh? You may depend upon it that the beast is either hiding something from us, or else she doesn't know herself what her husband looks like."

"Whatever the truth may be," said the elder sister, "we must ruin her as soon as possible. But if she really has never seen her husband, then he must be a god, and her baby will be a god too."

"If anything like that happens, which

Heaven forbid," said the younger, "I'll hang myself at once—I couldn't bear Psyche to mother an immortal. I think we have a clue now to the best way of tricking her. Meanwhile, what about calling on Father and Mother?"

They went to the palace, where they gave their parents an offhand greeting. The violence of their passions kept them awake all night. As soon as it was morning they hurried to the rock and floated down into the valley as usual with the help of the West Wind. Rubbing their eyelids hard until they managed to squeeze out a few tears, they went to Psyche and said: "Oh, sister, ignorance is indeed bliss! There you sit calmly and happily without the least suspicion of the terrible misfortune that has befallen you, while we are in absolute anguish about it. You see, we watch over your interests like true sis-

ters, and since we three have always shared the same sorrows and joys it would be wrong for us to hide your danger from you. It is this, that the husband who comes secretly gliding into your bed at night is an enormous snake, with widely gaping jaws, a body that could coil around you a dozen times and a neck swollen with deadly poison. Remember what Apollo's oracle said: that you were destined to marry a savage wild beast. Several of the farmers who go hunting in the woods around this place have met him coming home at nightfall from his feeding ground, and ever so many of the people in the nearest village have seen him swimming across the ford there. They all say that he won't pamper you much longer, but that when your nine months are nearly up he will eat you alive; apparently his favourite food is a woman far gone in pregnancy. So you had better make up your mind whether you will come away and live with us—we would do anything in the world to save you—or whether you prefer to stay here with this fiendish reptile until you finish up in his guts. Perhaps you're fascinated by living here alone with your voices all day, and at night having secret and disgusting relations with a poisonous snake; if so, you are welcome to the life, but at all events we have done our duty as affectionate sisters by warning you how it must end."

Poor silly Psyche was aghast at the dreadful news. She lost all control of herself, trembled, turned deathly pale, and forgetting all the warnings her husband had given her, and all her own promises, plunged headlong into the abyss of misfortune. She gasped out brokenly: "Dearest sisters, thank you for being so kind. You're quite right to warn me, and I believe that the people who told you were not making it up. The fact is, I have never seen my husband's face and haven't the least idea who he is or where he comes from. I only hear him speaking to me at night in whispers, and find it very hard to be married to someone who hates the light of day as much as he does. So I have every reason to suppose, as you do, that he must be some sort of monster. Besides, he is always giving me frightful warnings about what will happen if I try to see what he looks like. So please, if you can advise me what to do in this dreadful situation, tell me at once, like the dear sisters you are: otherwise, all the trouble you have been kind enough to take will be wasted."

The wicked women saw that Psyche's defences were down, and her heart laid open to their attacks. They pressed their advantage savagely. The younger said: "Blood is thicker than water; the thought of your danger makes us forget our own. We two have talked the matter over countless times since yesterday and have come to the conclusion that you have only one chance of saving yourself. It is this. Get hold of a very sharp carving knife, make it sharper still by stropping it on your palm, then hide it somewhere on your side of the bed. Also, get hold of a lamp, have it filled full of oil, trim the wick carefully, light it and hide it behind the bedroom tapestry. Do all this with the greatest secrecy and when the monster visits you as usual, wait until he is stretched out at full length, and you know by his deep breathing that he's fast asleep. Then slip out of bed with the knife in your hand and tiptoe barefooted to the place where you have hidden the lamp. Finally, with its light to assist you, perform your noble deed, plunge the knife down with all your strength at the nape of the creature's poisonous neck, and cut off his head. We promise to stand close by and keep careful watch. The moment you have saved yourself by killing it, we shall come running in and help you to get away at once with all your treasure. After that, we'll marry you to a decent human being."

When they saw that Psyche was now determined to follow their suggestion, they went quietly off, terrified to be anywhere near her when the catastrophe came; they were helped up to the rock by the West Wind, ran back to their ships as fast as they could and sailed off at once.

Psyche was left alone, except in so far as a woman who had decided to kill her husband is haunted by the Furies. Her mind was as restless as a stormy sea. When she first began making preparations for her crime, her resolve was firm; but presently she wavered and started worrying about what would happen if she succeeded and what would happen if she failed. She hurried, then she dawdled, not feeling quite sure whether after all she was doing the right thing, then got furiously angry again. The strange part of the story is that though she loathed the idea of sleeping with a poisonous snake, she was still in love with her husband. However, as the evening drew on, she finally made up her mind and hurriedly got the lamp and carving knife ready.

Night fell, and her husband came to bed, and as soon as they had finished kissing and embracing each other, he fell fast asleep. Psyche was not naturally either very strong or very brave, but the cruel power of fate made a virago of her. Holding the carving knife in a murderous grip, she uncovered the lamp and let its light shine on the bed.

At once the secret was revealed. There lay the gentlest and sweetest of all wild creatures, Cupid himself, the beautiful Love-god, and at sight of him the flame of the lamp spurted joyfully up and the knife turned its edge for shame.

Psyche was terrified. She lost all control of her senses, and pale as death, fell trembling to her knees, where she desperately tried to hide

the knife by plunging it in her own heart. She would have succeeded, too, had the knife not shrunk from the crime and twisted itself out of her hand. Faint and unnerved though she was, she began to feel better as she stared at Cupid's divine beauty: his golden hair, washed in nectar and still scented with it, thick curls straying over white neck and flushed checks and falling prettily entangled on either side of his head—hair so bright that the flame of the lamp winked in the radiant light reflected from it. At his shoulders grew soft wings of the purest white, and though they were at rest, the tender down fringing the feathers quivered naughtily all the time. The rest of his body was so smooth and beautiful that Venus could never have been ashamed to acknowledge him as her son. At the foot of the bed lay this great god's bow, quiver and arrows.

Psyche's curiosity could be satisfied only by a close examination of her husband's sacred weapons. She pulled an arrow out of the quiver and touched the point with the tip of her thumb to try its sharpness; but her hand was trembling and she pressed too hard. The skin was pierced and out came a drop or two of blood. So Psyche accidently fell in love with Love. Burning with greater passion for Cupid even than before, she flung herself panting upon him, desperate with desire, and smothered him with kisses; her one fear now being that he would wake too soon.

While she clung to him, utterly bewildered with delight, the lamp which she was still holding, whether from treachery or from envy, or because it longed as it were to touch and kiss such a marvellously beautiful body, spurted a drop of scalding oil on the God's right shoulder. What a bold and impudent lamp, what a worthless vessel at the altar of Love—for the first lamp was surely invented by some lover who wished to prolong all night the passionate delights of his eye—so to scorch the God of all fire! Cupid sprang up in pain, and taking in the whole disgraceful scene at a glance, spread his wings and flew off without a word; but not before the poor girl had seized his right leg with both hands and clung to it. She looked very queer, carried up like that through the cloudy sky; but soon her strength failed her and she tumbled down to earth again.

Cupid did not desert her immediately, but

alighted on the top of a cypress near by, where he stood reproaching her. "Oh, silly, foolish Psyche, it was for your sake that I disobeyed the orders of my mother Venus! She told me to inflame you with passion for some utterly worthless man, but I preferred to fly down from Heaven and become your lover myself. I know only too well that I acted thoughtlessly, and now look at the result! Cupid, the famous archer, wounds himself with one of his own arrows and marries a girl who mistakes him for a monster; she tries to chop off his head and darken the eyes that have beamed such love upon her. This was the danger of which I warned you again and again, gently begging you to be on your guard. As for those sisters of yours who turned you against me and gave you such damnable advice, I'll very soon be avenged on them. But your punishment will simply be that I'll fly away from you." He soared up into the air and was gone.

Psyche lay motionless on the ground, following him with her eyes and moaning bitterly. When the steady beat of his wings had carried him clean out of her sight, she climbed up the bank of a river that flowed close by and flung herself into the water. But the kindly river, out of respect for the god whose warm power is felt as much by water-creatures as by beasts and birds, washed her ashore with a gentle wave and laid her high and dry on the flowery turf.

Pan, the goat-legged country god, happened to be sitting near by, caressing the mountain nymph Echo and teaching her to repeat all sorts of pretty songs. A flock of she-goats roamed around, browsing greedily on the grass. Pan was already aware of Psyche's misfortune, so he gently beckoned to the desolate girl and did what he could to comfort her. "Pretty dear," he said soothingly. "Though I'm only an old, old shepherd and very much of a countryman, I have picked up a good deal of experience in my time. So if I am right in my conjecture, or my divination as sensible people would call it— your unsteady walk, your pallor, your constant sighs, and your sad eyes show that you're desperately in love. Listen: make no further attempt at suicide by leaping from a precipice, or doing anything else violent. Stop crying, try to be cheerful, and open your heart to Cupid, the greatest of us gods; he's a thoroughly spoilt young fellow whom you must humour by praying to him only in the gentlest, sweetest language."

It is very lucky to be addressed by Pan, but Psyche made no reply. She merely curtseyed dutifully and went on. She trudged along the road by the river for awhile, until for some reason or other she decided to follow a lane that led off it. Towards evening it brought her to a city of which she soon found out that her eldest sister was the queen. She announced her arrival at the palace and was at once admitted.

After an exchange of embraces, the queen asked Psyche why she had come. Psyche answered: "You remember your advice about that carving knife and the monstrous snake who pretended to be my husband and was going to swallow me? Well, I took it, but no sooner had I shone my lamp on the bed than I saw a marvellous sight: Venus's divine son, Cupid himself, lying there in tranquil sleep. The joy and relief were too great for me. I quite lost my head and didn't know how to satisfy my longing for him; but then, by a dreadful accident, a drop of burning oil from the lamp spurted on his shoulder. The pain woke him at once. When he saw me holding the lamp and the knife, he shouted: 'Wicked woman, out of this bed at once! I divorce you here and now. I am going to marry your eldest sister instead.' Then he called for the West Wind, who blew me out of the palace and landed me here."

Psyche had hardly finished her story before her sister, madly jealous of her for having been in bed with a god and burning with desire to have the same experience, rushed off to her husband with a story that her parents were dead, and that she must sail home at once. Off she went, and when at last she reached the rock, though another wind altogether was blowing, she shouted confidently: "Here I come, Cupid, a woman worthy of your love. West Wind, convey your mistress to the Palace at once!" Then she took a headlong leap; but she never reached the valley, either dead or alive, because the rocks cut her to pieces as she fell and scattered her flesh and guts all over the mountainside. So she got what she deserved, and the birds and beasts feasted on her remains.

Psyche wandered on and on until she came to another city, where the other sister was queen, and told her the same story. The wicked woman, wishing to supplant Psyche in Cupid's love, set sail at once, hurried to the rock, leaped off it and died in exactly the same way.

III

PSYCHE continued on her travels through country after country, searching for Cupid; but he was in Heaven, lying in bed in his mother's royal suite, groaning for pain. Meanwhile a white gull, of the sort that skims the surface of the sea flapping the waves with its wings, dived down into the water; there it met Venus, who was enjoying a dip, and brought her the news that her son Cupid was confined to bed by a severe and painful burn, from which it was doubtful whether he would recover. It told her, too, that every sort of scandal about the Venus family was going around. People were saying that her son had flown down to some mountain or other for an indecent affair with a girl, and that she herself had abandoned her divine tasks and gone off for a seaside holiday. "The result is," screamed the gull, "that Pleasure, Grace and Wit have disappeared from the earth and everything there has become ugly, dull and slovenly. Nobody bothers any longer about his wife, his friends or his children; and the whole system of human love is in such complete disorder that it is now considered disgusting for anyone to show even natural affection."

This talkative, meddlesome bird succeeded in setting Venus against her son. She grew very angry and cried: "So my promising lad has already taken a mistress, has he? Here, gull— you seem to be the only creature left with any true affection for me—tell me, do you know the name of the creature who has seduced my poor simple boy? Is she one of the Nymphs, or one of the Hours, or one of the Muses, or one of my own train of Graces?"

The gull was very ready to spread the scandal it had picked up. "I cannot say for certain, Your Majesty, but unless my memory is playing me tricks, I think the story is that your son has fallen desperately in love with a human named Psyche."

Venus was absolutely furious. "What! With her, of all women? With Psyche, the usurper of my beauty, the rival of my glory? This is worse and worse. It was through me that he got to know the girl. Does the impudent young wretch take me for a procuress?"

She rose from the sea at once and hurried aloft to her golden room, where she found

Cupid lying ill in bed, as the gull had told her. As she entered she bawled out at the top of her voice: "Now *is* this decent behaviour? A fine credit you are to your divine family and a fine reputation you're building up for yourself. You trample your mother's orders underfoot as though she had no authority over you whatsoever, and instead of tormenting her enemy with a dishonourable passion, as you were ordered to do, you have the impudence to sleep with the girl yourself. At your age, you lecherous little beast! I suppose you thought that I'd be delighted to have her for a daughter-in-law, eh? And I suppose you also thought, you scamp, you debauched detestable brat, that you're my heir and that I'm past the age of child-bearing! Please understand that I'm quite capable of having another son, if I please, and a far better one than you, and quite prepared to disinherit you in his favour. However, to make you feel the disgrace still more keenly, I think I'll legally adopt the son of one of my slaves and hand over to him your wings, torch, bow and arrows, which you have been using in ways for which I never intended them. And I have every right to do that, because not one of them was supplied by your father Vulcan. The fact is that you have been mischievous from your earliest years and always delighted in hurting people. You have often had the bad manners to shoot at your elders, and as for me, your mother, you shame me before the whole world day after day, you matricidal wretch, by sticking me full of your horrible little arrows. You sneer at me and call me 'the widow,' I suppose because your father and I are no longer on speaking terms, and show not the slightest respect for your brave, invincible stepfather Mars; in fact, you do your best to annoy me by setting him after other women and making me madly jealous. But you'll soon be sorry that you played all those tricks; I warn you that this marriage of yours is going to leave a sour, bitter taste in your mouth."

He did not answer, so she complained to herself in an undertone: "This is all very well, but everyone is laughing at me and I haven't the faintest idea what to do or where to go. How in the world am I to catch and cage the nasty little lizard? I suppose I'd better go for help to old Sobriety to whom I've always been so dreadfully rude for the sake of this spoilt son of mine. Must I really have anything to do with that dowdy, countrified old bore, my natural foe? The idea makes me shudder, yet revenge is sweet from whatever quarter it comes. Yes, I fear that she's the only person who can do anything for me. She'll give the little beast the thrashing of his life; confiscate his quiver, blunt his arrows, tear the string off his bow and quench his torch. Worse than that, she'll shave off his golden hair, which I used to curl so carefully with my own hands, and clip those lovely wings of his which I once whitened with the dazzling milk of my own breast. When that's been done, perhaps I'll feel a little better."

She rushed off again and at once ran into her stepmother Juno and her aunt Ceres, who noticed how angry she looked and asked her why she was spoiling the beauty of her bright eyes with so sullen a frown. "Thank goodness I met you," she answered. "I needed you to calm me down. There is something you can do for me, if you'll be kind enough. Please make careful enquiries for the whereabouts of a runaway creature called Psyche—I'm sure you must have heard all about her and the family scandal she's caused by her affair with . . . with you know whom!"

Of course, they knew all about it, and tried to soothe her fury. "Darling," Juno said, "you mustn't take this too much to heart. Why try to thwart his pleasures and kill the girl with whom he's fallen in love? What terrible sin has he committed? It is no crime, surely, to sleep with a pretty girl?"

And Ceres said: "Darling, you imagine that he's still only a boy because he carries his years so gracefully, but you simply must realize that he's a young man now. Have you forgotten his age? And, really, Juno and I think it very strange that, as a mother and a woman of the world, you persist in poking your nose into what is really his own business, and that when you catch him out in a love affair you blame the poor darling for those very talents and inclinations that he inherits directly from yourself. What god or man will have any patience with you, you go about all the time waking sexual desire in people but at the same time try to repress similar feelings in your own son? Is it really your intention to close down the sole existing factory of woman's universal weakness?"

The Goddesses were not quite honest in their defence of Cupid: they were afraid of his arrows and thought it wiser to speak well of him even when he was not about. Venus, seeing that they refused to take a serious view of her wrongs, indignantly turned her back on them and hurried off again to the sea.

Meanwhile, Psyche was restlessly wandering about day and night in search for her husband. However angry he might be, she hoped to make him relent either by coaxing him in their own private love-language or by going down on her knees in abject repentance. One day she noticed a temple on the top of a steep hill. She said to herself: "I wonder if my husband is there?" So she walked quietly towards the hill, her heart full of love and hope, and reached the temple with some difficulty, after climbing ridge after ridge. But when she arrived at the sacred couch she found it heaped with votive gifts of wheat-sheaves, wheat-chaplets and ears of barley, also

sickles and other harvest implements; but all scattered about untidily, as though flung down at the close of a hot summer day by careless reapers.

She began to sort all these things carefully, and arrange them in their proper places, feeling that she must behave respectfully towards every deity whose temple she happened to visit and implore the help of the whole Heavenly family one by one. The temple belonged to the generous Goddess Ceres, who saw her busily at work and called out from afar: "Oh, you poor Psyche! Venus is furious and searching everywhere for you. She wants to be cruelly revenged on you. I am surprised that you can spare the time to look after my affairs for me, or think of anything at all but your own safety."

Psyche's hair streamed across the temple

floor as she prostrated herself at the Goddess's feet, which she wetted with her tears. She implored her protection: "I beseech you, Goddess, by the corn-stalks in your hand, by the happy ceremony of harvest-home, by the secret contents of the wicker baskets carried in your procession, by the winged dragons of your chariot, by the furrows of Sicily from which a cruel god once ravished your daughter Proserpine, by the wheels of his chariot, by the earth that closed upon her, by her dark descent and gloomy wedding, by her happy torch-lit return to earth, and by the other mysteries which Eleusis, your Attic sanctuary, silently conceals:—help me, oh please help your unhappy suppliant Psyche. Allow me, just for a few days, to hide myself under that stack of wheat-sheaves, until the great Goddess's rage has had time to cool down; or if not for so long as that, at least let me have a short rest, because, honestly, I am very, very tired, and haven't stopped travelling for a moment since I set out."

Ceres answered: "Your tears and prayers go straight to my heart, and I would dearly love to help you; but the truth is that I can't afford to offend my niece. She has been one of my best friends for ages and ages and really has a very good heart when you get to know her. You'd better leave this temple at once and think yourself lucky that I don't have you placed under arrest."

Psyche went away, twice as sad as she had come: she had never expected such a rebuff. But soon she saw below her in the valley another beautiful temple in the middle of a dark sacred grove. She feared to miss any chance, even a remote one, of putting things right for herself, so she went down to implore the protection of the deity of the place, whoever it might be. She saw various splendid offerings hanging from branches of the grove and from the temple door-posts; among them were rich garments embroidered with gold letters that spelt out the name of the goddess to whom all were dedicated, namely Juno, and recorded the particular favours which she had granted their donors.

Psyche fell on her knees, wiped away her tears, and embracing the temple altar, still warm from a recent sacrifice, began to pray. "Sister and wife of great Jupiter, I cannot tell where you may be at the moment. You may be residing in one of your ancient temples on Samos—the Samians boast that you were born in their island and spent your whole impassioned childhood there. Or you may be visiting your happy city of Carthage on its high hill, where you are adored as a virgin travelling across Heaven in a lion-drawn chariot. Or you may be watching over the famous walls of Argos, past which the river Inachus flows, where you are adored as the Queen of Heaven, the Thunderer's bride. Wherever you are, you whom the whole East venerates as Zygia the Goddess of Marriage, and the whole West as Lucina, Goddess of Childbirth, I appeal to you now as Juno the Protectress: I beg you to watch over me in my overwhelming misfortune, and rescue me from the dangers that threaten me. You see, Goddess, I am very, very tired, and very, very frightened and I know that you're always ready to help women who are about to have babies, if they get into any sort of trouble."

Juno appeared in all her august glory and said: "My dear, I should be only too pleased to help you, but unfortunately divine etiquette forbids. I can't possibly go against the wishes of Venus, who married my son Vulcan, you know, and whom I have always loved as though she were my own child. Besides, I am forbidden by law—one of the Fabian laws—to harbour any fugitive slave-girl without her owner's consent."

Psyche was distressed by this second shipwreck of her hopes, and felt quite unable to go on looking for her winged husband. She gave up all hope of safety and said to herself: "Where in the world, or out of it, can I turn for help, now that even these powerful goddesses will do nothing for me but express their sympathy? My feet are so tangled in the snares of fate that it seems useless to ask them to take me anywhere else. Where is there a building in which I can hide myself from the watchful eyes of great Venus, even with all doors and windows locked? The fact is, my dear Psyche, that you must borrow a little male courage, you must boldly renounce all idle hopes of escape and make a voluntary surrender to your sovereign mistress. It may be too late, but you must at least try to calm her rage by submissive behaviour. Besides, after this long, useless search, you have quite a good chance of finding your husband at your mother-in-law's house."

Psyche's decision to do her duty was risky and even suicidal, but she prepared herself for it by considering what sort of appeal she ought to make to her Mistress.

Venus meanwhile had declined to use any human agencies in her search for Psyche and returned to Heaven, where she ordered her chariot to be got ready. It was of burnished gold, with coach-work of such exquisite filigree that its intrinsic value was negligible compared with its value as a work of art. It had been her husband Vulcan's wedding present to her. Four white doves from the flock in constant attendance on her flew happily forward and offered their rainbow-coloured necks to the jewelled harness and, when Venus mounted, drew the chariot along at a spanking rate. Behind, flew a crowd of naughty sparrows and other little birds that sang very sweetly in announcement of the Goddess's arrival.

Now the clouds vanished, the sky opened and the high upper air received her joyfully. Her singing retinue were not in the least afraid of swooping eagles or greedy hawks, and she drove straight to the royal citadel of Jupiter, where she demanded the immediate services of Mercury, the town-crier of Heaven, in a matter of great urgency. When Jupiter nodded his sapphire brow in assent, Venus was delighted; she retired from his presence and gave Mercury, who was now accompanying her, careful instructions. "Brother from Arcady, you know I have never in my life undertaken any business at all without your assistance, and you know how long I have been without news of my runaway slave girl. So you simply must make a public announcement offering a reward to the person who finds her, and insist on my orders

being obeyed at once. Her person must be accurately described so that nobody will be able to plead ignorance as an excuse for harbouring her. Here is her dossier; Psyche is the name, and all particulars are included."

She handed him a little book and immediately went home. Mercury did as he was told. He went from country to country crying out: "Oyez, oyez! If any person can apprehend and seize the person of a runaway princess, one of the Lady Venus's slave-girls, by name PSYCHE, or give any information that will lead to her discovery, let such a person go to Mercury, Town-crier of Heaven, in his temple just outside the precincts of Our Lady of the Myrtles, Aventine Hill, Rome. The reward offered is as follows: seven sweet kisses from the mouth of the said Venus herself, and one exquisitely delicious thrust of her honeyed tongue between his pursed lips."

A jealous competitive spirit naturally fired all mankind when they heard this reward announced, and it was this that put an immediate end to Psyche's hesitation. She was already near her mistress's gate when she was met by one of the household, named Old Habit, who screamed out at once at the top of her voice: "You wicked slut, you! So you've discovered at last that you have a mistress, eh? But don't pretend, you brazen-faced thing, that you haven't heard of the huge trouble that you've caused us in our search for you. Well, I'm glad you've fallen into my hands, not some other slave's, because you're safe here—safe in the jaws of Hell, and there won't be any delay in your punishment either, you obstinate, impertinent baggage!" She twisted her fingers in Psyche's hair and dragged her into Venus's presence, though she came along willingly enough.

Venus burst into the hysterical laugh of a woman who is desperately angry. She shook her head menacingly and scratched her ear—the right ear, behind which the Throne of Vengeance is said to be situated. "Ah," she cried, "so you condescend to pay your respects to your mother-in-law, is that it? Or perhaps you have come to visit your husband's sick-bed, hearing that he's still dangerously ill from the burn you gave him? But make yourself at home. I promise you the sort of welcome that a good mother-in-law is bound to give her son's wife." She clapped her hands for her slaves, Anxiety and Grief, and when they ran up, gave Psyche over to them for punishment. They led her off, flogged her cruelly and tortured her in other ways besides, after which they brought her back to Venus's presence.

Once more Venus yelled with laughter: "Just look at her!" she cried. "Look at the whore! That big belly of hers makes me feel quite sorry for her. By Heaven, it wrings my grandmotherly heart! Grandmother, indeed! How wonderful to be made a grandmother at my time of life! And to think that the son of this disgusting slave will be called Venus's own grandchild! No, but of course that is nonsense. A marriage between a god and a mortal, celebrated in the depth of the country without witnesses and lacking even the consent of the bride's father, can't possibly be recognized at Law; your child will be a bastard, my girl, even if I permit you to bring it into the world."

With this, she flew at poor Psyche, tore her clothes to shreds, pulled out handfuls of her hair, then grabbed her by the shoulders and shook her until she nearly shook her head off, giving her a terrible time. Next she called for quantities of wheat, barley, millet, lentils, beans and the seeds of poppy and vetch, and mixed them all together into a huge heap. "You look such a dreadful sight, slave," she said, "that the only way that you are ever likely to get a lover is by hard work. So now I'll test you myself, to find out whether you're industrious. Do you see this pile of seeds all mixed together? Sort out the different kinds, stack them in separate little heaps, and prove that you're quick-fingered by getting every grain in its right place before nightfall." Without another word, she flew off to attend some wedding breakfast or other.

Psyche made no attempt to set about her stupendous task, but sat gazing dumbly at it, until a very small ant, one of the country sort, happened to pass and realized what was going on. Pity for Psyche as wife of the mighty God of Love set the little thing shrieking wild curses at the cruel mother-in-law and scurrying about to round up every ant in the district. "Take pity on her, sisters, take pity on this pretty girl, you busy children of the generous Earth. She's the wife of Love himself and her life is in great danger. Quick, quick, to the rescue!"

They came rushing up as fast as their six legs would carry them, wave upon wave of ants, and began working furiously to sort the pile out, grain by grain. Soon they had arranged it all tidily in separate heaps, and run off again at once.

Venus returned that evening, a little drunk, smelling strongly of aphrodisiac ointments, and simply swathed in rose-wreaths. When she saw with what prodigious speed Psyche had finished the task, she said: "You didn't do a hand's stroke yourself, you wicked thing. This is the work of someone whom you have bewitched, poor fellow! but you'll be 'poor fellow' too, before I have done." She threw her part of a coarse loaf and went to bed.

Meanwhile she had confined Cupid to his bedroom, partly to prevent him from playing his usual naughty tricks and so making his injury worse; partly to keep him away from his sweetheart. So the lovers spent a miserable night, unable to visit each other, although under the same roof.

As soon as the Goddess of Dawn had set

her team moving across the sky, Venus called Psyche and said: "Do you see the grove fringing the bank of that stream over there, with fruit bushes hanging low over the water? Shining golden sheep are wandering about in it, without a shepherd to look after them. I want you to fetch me a hank of their precious wool, and I don't care how you get it."

Psyche rose willingly enough, but with no intention of obeying Venus's orders: she had made up her mind to throw herself in the stream and so end her sorrows. But a green reed, of the sort used in Pan's pipes, was blown upon by some divine breeze and whispered to her: "Wait, Psyche, wait! I know what dreadful sorrows you have suffered, but you must not pollute these sacred waters by a suicide. And, another thing, you must not go into the grove, to risk your life among those dangerous sheep; not yet. The heat of the sun so infuriates the beasts that they kill any human being who ventures among them. Either they gore them with their sharp horns, or butt them to death with their stony foreheads or bite them with their poisonous teeth. Wait, Psyche, wait until the afternoon wears to a close, and the serene whispers of these waters lull them asleep. Hide meanwhile under that tall plane-tree who drinks the same water as I do, and as soon as the sheep calm down, go into the grove and gather the wisps of golden wool that you'll find sticking on every briar there."

It was a simple, kindly reed and Psyche took its advice, which proved to be sound: that evening she was able to return to Venus with a whole lapful of the delicate golden wool. Yet even her performance of this second dangerous task did not satisfy the Goddess, who frowned and told her with a cruel smile: "Someone has been helping you again, that's quite clear. But now I'll put your courage and prudence to a still severer test. Do you see the summit of that high mountain over there? You'll find that a dark-coloured stream cascades down its precipitous sides into a gorge below and then floods the Stygian marshes and feeds the hoarse River of Wailing. Here is a little jar. Go off at once and bring it back to me brimful of ice-cold water fetched from the very middle of the stream at the point where it bursts out of the rock."

She gave Psyche a jar of polished crystal and packed her off with renewed threats of what would happen if she came back empty-handed.

Psyche started at once for the top of the mountain, which was called Aroanius, thinking that there at least she would find a means of ending her wretched life. As she came near she saw what a stupendously dangerous and difficult task had been set her. The dreadful waters of the Styx burst out from half-way up an enormously tall, steep, slippery precipice; cascaded down into a narrow conduit which they had hollowed for themselves in the course of centuries; and flowed unseen into the gorge below. On both sides of their outlet she saw fierce dragons crawling, never asleep, always on guard with unwinking eyes, and stretching their long necks over the sacred water. And the waters sang as they rolled along, varying the words every now and then: "Be off! Be off!" and "What do you wish, wish, wish? Look! Look!"

and "What are you at, are you at? Care, take care!" "Off with you, off with you, off with you! Death! Death!"

Psyche stood still as stone, her mind far away: the utter impossibility of escaping alive from the trap that Venus had set for her was so overwhelming that she could no longer even relieve herself by tears—that last comfort of women when things go wrong with them. But the kind, sharp eyes of Providence notice when innocent souls are in trouble. At her suggestion Jupiter's royal bird, the rapacious eagle, suddenly sailed down to her from Heaven. He gratefully remembered the ancient debt that he owed to Cupid for having helped him to carry Ganymede, the beautiful Phrygian prince, up to Heaven to become Jupiter's cup-bearer; and since Psyche was Cupid's wife he screamed down at her: "Silly, simple, inexperienced Psyche, how can you ever hope to steal one drop of this frightfully sacred stream? Surely you have heard that Jupiter himself fears the waters of Styx, and that just as you swear by the Blessed Gods, so they swear by the Sovereign Styx. But let me take that little jar." He quickly snatched it from her grasp and soared off on his strong wings, steering a zigzag course between the two rows of furious fangs and vibrating three-forked tongues, until he reached the required spot. The stream was reluctant to give up its water and warned him to escape while he still could, but he explained that the Goddess Venus wanted the water and that she had commissioned him to fetch it; a story which carried some weight with the stream. He filled the jar with the water and brought it safely back to the delighted Psyche.

She returned with it to Venus but could not appease her fury even with this latest success. Venus was resolved to set a still more outrageous test, and said with a sweet smile that seemed to spell her complete ruin: "You must be a witch, a very clever, very wicked witch, else you could never have carried out my orders so exactly. But I have still one more task for you to perform, my dear girl. Please take this box and go down to the Underworld to the death-palace of Pluto. Hand it to Queen Proserpine and say: 'The Lady Venus's compliments, and will you please send this box back to her with a little of your beauty in it, not very much but enough to last for at least one short day. She has had to make such a drain on her own store as a result of sitting up at night with her sick son that she has none left.' Then come back with the box at once, because I must use her make-up before I appear at the Olympic Theatre tonight."

This seemed the end of everything, since her orders were to go down to the Underworld of Tartarus. Psyche saw that she was openly and undisguisedly being sent to her death. She went at once to a high tower, deciding that her straightest and easiest way to the Underworld was to throw herself down from it. But the tower suddenly broke into human speech: "Poor child," it said, "do you really mean to commit suicide by jumping down from me? How rash of you to lose hope just before the end of your trials. Don't you realize that as soon as the breath is out of your body you will indeed go right down to the depths of Tartarus, but that once you take that way there's no hope of return? Listen to me. The famous Greek city of Lacedaemon is not far from here. Go there at once and ask to be directed to Taenarus, which is rather an out-of-the-way place to find. It's on a peninsula to the south. Once you get there you'll find one of the ventilation holes of the Underworld. Put your head through it and you'll see a road running downhill, but there'll be no traffic on it. Climb through at once and the road will lead you straight to Pluto's palace. But don't forget to take with you two pieces of barley bread soaked in honey water, one in each hand, and two coins in your mouth.

"When you have gone a good way along the

road you'll meet a lame ass loaded with wood, and its lame driver will ask you to hand him some pieces of rope for tying up part of the load which the ass has dropped. Pass him by in silence. Then hurry forward until you reach the river of the dead, where Charon will at once ask you for his fee and ferry you across in his patched boat among crowds of ghosts. It seems that the God Avarice lives thereabouts, because neither Charon nor his great father Pluto does anything for nothing. (A poor man on the point of death is expected to have his passage-fee ready; but if he can't get hold of a coin, he isn't allowed to achieve true death, but must wander about disconsolately forever on this side of Styx.) Anyhow, give the dirty ruffian one of your coins, but let him take it from your mouth, not from your hand. While you are being ferried across the sluggish stream, the corpse of an old man will float by; he will raise a putrid hand and beg you to haul him into the boat. But you must be careful not to yield to any feeling of pity for him; that is forbidden. Once ashore, you will meet three women some distance away from the bank. They will be weaving cloth and will ask you to help them. To touch the cloth is also forbidden. All these apparitions, and others like them, are snares set for you by Venus; her object is to make you let go one of the sops you are carrying, and you must understand that the loss of even one of them would be fatal—it would prevent your return to this world. They are for you to give to Cerberus, the huge, fierce, formidable hound with three heads on three necks, all barking in unison, who terrifies the dead; though of course

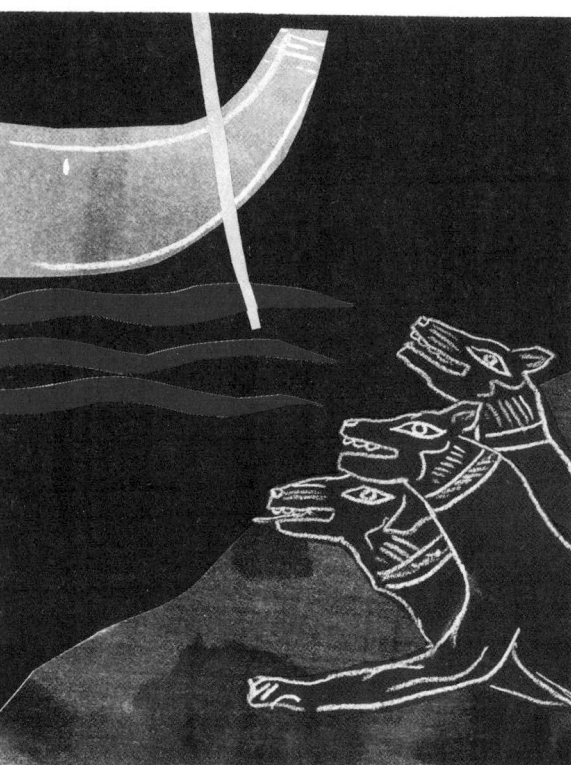

the dead have no need to be frightened by him because they are only shadows and he can't injure shadows.

"Cerberus keeps perpetual guard at the threshold of Proserpine's dark palace, the desolate place where she lives with her husband Pluto. Throw him one of your sops and you'll find it easy to get past him into the presence of Proserpine herself. She'll give you a warm welcome, offer you a cushioned chair and have you brought a magnificent meal. But sit on the ground, ask for a piece of common bread and eat nothing else. Then deliver your message, and she'll give you what you came for.

"As you go out, throw the cruel dog the remaining sop as a bribe to let you pass; then pay the greedy ferryman the remaining coin for your return fare across the river, and when you're safely on the other bank follow the road back until you see once again the familiar constellations of Heaven. One last, important warning; be careful not to open or even look at the box you carry back; that hidden receptacle of divine beauty is not for you to explore."

It was a kind and divinely inspired tower and Psyche took its advice. She went at once to Taenarus where, armed with the coins and the two sops, she ran down the road to the Underworld. She passed in silence by the lame man with the lame ass, paid Charon the first coin, stopped her ears to the entreaties of the floating corpse, refused to be taken in by the appeal of the spinning women, pacified the dreadful dog with the first sop and entered Proserpine's palace. There she refused the comfortable chair and the tempting meal, sat humbly at Proserpine's feet, content with a crust of common bread, and finally delivered her message. Proserpine secretively filled the box, shut it and returned it to her; then Psyche stopped the dog's barking with the second sop, paid Charon with the second coin and returned from the Underworld, feeling in far better health and spirits than while on her way down there. When she saw the daylight again she offered up a prayer of praise for its loveliness. Though she was in a hurry to complete her errand she foolishly allowed her curiosity to get the better of her. She said to herself: "I should be a fool to carry this little boxful of divine beauty without borrowing a tiny touch of it for my own use: I must do everything possible to please my beautiful lover."

She opened the box, but it contained no

beauty nor anything else, so far as she saw: but out crept a truly Stygian sleep which seized her, and wrapped her in a dense cloud of drowsiness. She fell prostrate and lay there like a corpse, the open box beside her.

Cupid, now recovered from his injury and unable to bear Psyche's absence a moment longer, flew out through the narrow window of the bedroom where his mother had been holding him a prisoner. His wings, invigorated by their long rest, carried him faster than ever before. He hurried to Psyche, carefully brushed away the cloud of sleep from her body and shut it up again in its box, then roused her with a harmless prick of an arrow. "Poor girl," he said, "your curiosity has once more nearly ruined you. Hurry now and complete the task which my mother set you; and I'll see to everything else." He flew off, and she sprang up at once to deliver Proserpine's present to Venus.

But Cupid, who had fallen more deeply in love with Psyche than ever and was alarmed by his mother's sudden conversion to respectability, returned to his naughty tricks. He flew at great speed to the very highest heaven and flung himself as a suppliant at Jupiter's feet, where he pleaded his case. Jupiter pinched his handsome cheeks and kissed his hand. Then he said: "My masterful child, you never pay me the respect which has been decreed me by the Council of Gods, and you're always shooting your arrows into my divine heart—the very seat of the laws that govern the four elements and all the constellations of the sky. Often you defile it with mortal love affairs, contrary to the Laws of Heaven, the Julian edict against adultery, and public peace, injuring my reputation and authority by involving me in sordid love intrigues and transmogrifying my serene appearance into that of serpent, fire, wild beast, bird or farmyard bull. Nevertheless, I can't forget how often I've nursed you on my knees and how softhearted I can be, so I'll do whatever you ask. But please realize that you must protect yourself against a Certain Person who might envy you your beautiful wife, and at the same time reward him for what he's going to do for you; so I advise you to introduce me to whatever other girl of really outstanding beauty happens to be about on the earth today."

Then he ordered Mercury to call a Council of All Heavens, with a penalty of ten thousand drachmae for non-appearance. Everyone was afraid to be fined such a sum, so the Celestial Theatre filled up at once, and Almighty Jupiter from his sublime throne read the following address:

Right honourable gods and goddesses whose names are registered in the White Roll of the Muses, you all know the young fellow over there whom I have brought up from boyhood and whose passionate nature must, in my opinion, be curbed in some way or other. It is enough to remind you of the daily complaints that come in of his provoking someone or other to adultery or a similar crime. Well, I have decided that we must stop the young rascal from doing anything of the sort again by fastening the fetters of marriage securely upon him. He has found and seduced a pretty girl called Psyche, and my sentence is that he must have her, hold her, possess her and cherish her from this time forth and for evermore.

Then he turned to Venus: "My dear, you have no occasion to be sad, or ashamed that your rank and station in Heaven have been disgraced by your son's match; for I'll see that the marriage is one between social equals, perfectly legitimate and in complete accordance with civil law." He ordered Mercury to fetch Psyche at once and escort her into his presence. When she arrived he took a cup of nectar and handed it to her. "Drink, Psyche, and become an immortal," he said. "Cupid will now never

fly away from your arms, but must remain your lawful husband for ever."

Presently a great wedding breakfast was prepared. Cupid reclined in the place of honour with Psyche's head resting on his breast; Jupiter was placed next, with Juno in the same comfortable position, and then all the other gods and goddesses in order of seniority. Jupiter was served with nectar and ambrosia by apple-cheeked Ganymede, his personal cup-bearer; Bacchus attended to everyone else. Vulcan was the chef; the Hours decorated the palace with red roses and other bridal flowers; the Graces sprinkled balsam water; the Muses chanted the marriage-hymn to the accompaniment of flute and pipe-music from the godlings Satyrus and Peniscus. Finally Apollo sang to his own lyre and the music was so sweet that Venus came forward and performed a lively step-dance in time to it. Psyche was properly married to Cupid and in due time she bore him her child, a daughter whose name was Pleasure.

SHAMBHALA CENTAUR EDITIONS are named for a classical modern typeface designed by the eminent American typographer Bruce Rogers. Modeled on a fifteenth-century Roman type, Centaur was originally an exclusive titling font for the Metropolitan Museum of Art, New York. The first book in which it appeared was Maurice de Guérin's *The Centaur*, printed in 1915. Until recently, Centaur type was available only for handset books printed on letterpress. Its elegance and clarity make it the typeface of choice for Shambhala Centaur Editions, which include outstanding classics of the world's literary and spiritual traditions.

Also in SHAMBHALA CENTAUR EDITIONS

Look! This Is Love: Poems of Rumi
Translated by Annemarie Schimmel

Narrow Road to the Interior
by Matsuo Bashō
Translated by Sam Hamill

Only Companion: Japanese Poems
of Love and Longing
Translated and edited by Sam Hamill